Shamrock Kisses

A High Five Novella
Book #3

By Serena Pier

First Edition January 2025.

Cover Image: Serena Pier LLC.

Interior Formatting: Brianna Cooper

To all the girls who want a nerd in the streets and a freak in the sheets, Patrick Nowak has arrived.

Content Warning

Alcohol Consumption, Anxiety, Discussions of Past Depression and Mental Health Struggles, Profanity, Sexually Explicit Content

Reading Order

***High Five Novella* Series:**

Part 1

Santa's Coming

Cupid's Shot

Shamrock Kisses

Part 2

Run Little Bunny
Releasing March 20, 2025

Falling For Red
Releasing June 5th, 2025

1

Patrick

Friday, March 14th

"Thanks for getting me out of Chicago for the weekend. Does it really get that crazy for St. Patrick's Day?" I ask my friend and co-worker, Brandon, as he drives us to Lake Geneva, Wisconsin, for the weekend. It will be good to get out of the city for a couple of days. To chill and unwind. Staring at a screen for nearly every waking minute can't be healthy. *I need a digital detox, and Brandon needs to reset after a big fight with his on-again, off-again girlfriend.*

"Yeah. Imagine being surrounded by thousands of suburbanites drinking green beer and puking it up in the street." Brandon's barely keeping his hand on the wheel of the Rivian SUV as the self-driving features guide us along the highway. I don't own a car—minimalism suits me.

"So, it's just us at your family's lake house?"

"Unless you find some townie," he teases.

"Good joke." It's emphasized by me reflexively pushing my glasses up my nose.

The idea of me finding a girl is absurd. I'm a nerd. The quiet coder who doesn't have a suave bone in his body.

Staring out the window, my mind drifts to the minor platform updates I need to push once we get to the lake house. I should try to make this weekend into a retreat and go to bed at a reasonable hour for the next couple of days. Staying up until four in the morning is another bad habit—especially when paired with late-night snacking.

"It's too cold to go boating," Brandon says, pulling me back to the present. "There are some great restaurants in town, though. But we'll probably spend most of our time on the property."

"I still can't believe your dad is Kent Dubois." *He's only a billionaire.*

We pull through a huge, ornate gate. Brandon's family's lake house is a mansion. I inwardly chuckle that they call this place a lake house. It's more like a resort.

Having grown up in Minnesota, I'm still getting used to Chicago's dynamics—especially how people "summer" as if it's a verb. I definitely wasn't raised thinking of seasons that way.

"Don't be so impressed by Kent," Brandon says. "This house is about all he's good for."

We've been friends for a little more than a year, both working for a crypto trading platform called Cryptoball. I'm learning his relationship with his dad is far from the one I have with mine. At least I still call my dad "Dad."

As we step inside, I take in the vast space—high ceilings, pristine surfaces—and immediately feel out of place in my hoodie and sweatpants. Before I can fully absorb the place, I notice a sweaty, beautiful brunette with a messy bun mopping the entryway. She looks embarrassed, pulling the earbuds from her ears. *Was that Wind Walkers I just heard blaring?*

"Sorry. We're running behind," she says, and I hear vacuums in the distance. "I usually have a team of four, but it's just me and two other girls today."

"All good," Brandon replies, adjusting the strap of his bag.

"I know your dad—"

"I'm not him," Brandon interrupts. "I don't mind seeing the help," he says with a laugh as if he understands the absurdity of the situation.

Her bright blue eyes meet my green ones, or at least meet my glasses. I feel like I'm being studied. Why is she staring at me so intently? Standing beside her, I realize she barely reaches my chest. At five-foot-ten, not exactly towering, but she's so petite I almost feel like a giant.

I smirk, checking her out before feeling embarrassed at how blatant I'm being. Brushing a hand through my messy brown hair, I hope I don't look as frazzled as I feel. Crumbs in my beard? I swipe at it, praying that's not why she's staring at me.

"Do you guys have any fun plans for the weekend?" she asks politely, looking back at Brandon. She's probably interested in him—his trust fund and effortless coolness. Not me, looking like I just crawled out of a hackathon in my hoodie.

Her cheeks are flushed, and my eyes, once again, have a mind of their own, checking her out. She's exactly my type—athletic but thick in all the right places. Meanwhile, I've got a few extra pounds I'd like to pretend are muscle, but who am I kidding? Too many late-night snacks while coding have added more bulk than I'd like.

Brandon shrugs. "We're planning on hanging around here."

"Well ..." She hesitates, glancing at me before continuing. Her crop top features the cover art from a Brand New album. I'm intrigued. I love that band, and the top highlights her tiny waist. Does she lift weights? Her strong thighs make me think so. I push down the thought of wanting to know what her ass looks like. "If you want to get out of the house, you should come to High Five tomorrow."

She smiles at me, and my heart rate spikes. Is this her way of saying she wants me to go there? Am I reading this situation right? She's way too hot for me.

"High Five?" Brandon asks. "The dive bar?"

"It used to be a dive bar," she says before looking back at me. "It has a new owner."

"Will there be green beer?" Brandon asks, laughing lightly.

"Oh no!" She giggles, and I find everything about her cute. For someone mopping floors, she's got an unshakable confidence, like she's totally comfortable being the coolest person in the room. She's got to be about my age, mid-to-late twenties. "The owner swears it'll be nothing like that. I believe the tagline is, 'All of the Guinness, None of the Sloppiness.'"

"Sounds fun," I say, staring into her eyes. The quiet coder with no game. That's me. Yet here I am, trying to flirt with a girl who's way out of my league.

"We'll see," Brandon says, his tone uninterested as he walks farther into the home.

Okay, I need to say something to her. Just something smooth. *You've got this. Don't blow it. Maybe something about beer ...*

"Good thing I like Guinness," I say softly, passing her and following Brandon. I can't believe I managed to flirt.

That was solid. I don't need to overanalyze it. But it was a good line.

"I'll be there with my friends," she says, holding my gaze before my eyes betray me, dropping to check out her ass. "It's always a good time." And damn, she's even more perfect from behind.

I wish I could just tell her I'll see her tomorrow, but I don't know if I can confirm. I need to talk to Brandon, and I really want to see her again.

Following him through the house, we stop at the panoramic windows overlooking the lake. "I get why this view costs thirty million," I say in awe.

"I love this house," Brandon says, smiling at the view.

"Should we go to that bar she mentioned?"

I want to go, but Brandon's been sober for a few years. I've been to bars with him before, so I know that's not an issue, but I don't want to assume.

"I don't know, man." He rubs the back of his neck. "That place holds some rough memories for me."

"All good. We can skip it." I should be a good friend. We didn't plan on girls being part of this weekend anyway.

"Come on." He laughs. "You're going!"

"I am?" I can't hold back my smile.

"You were really checking her out. You like her."

"That obvious?" I ask, feeling a bit nervous. "I thought I was keeping my cool."

"I don't know if I've ever seen you so stunned by a girl before." Brandon fist-bumps me. "Go flirt with her. Stop overthinking."

"How do you know I'm overthinking?"

"Because you're Patrick 'The Patch'—one of the smartest, most thoughtful people I know."

When was the last time I talked to a girl outside of work or gaming? Too long.

"I think her name is Rachel," Brandon says with a mild level of confidence. "She seems between us in age." Entrepreneurial. Cute." He raises a brow. "Short brunettes are great, but tall ones ..." He trails off, rolling his eyes. I wish he and his on-again, off-again girlfriend would just stay off.

"You know, not so funny story," Brandon starts, "our last cleaning company stole a figurine worth a quarter of a million dollars."

"Fuck."

"It was insured, no big deal, but we had to find a new company. Usually, the house manager handles that, but Kent insisted on hiring the next one. She came over, they exchanged a few sentences, and he hired her."

She owns a cleaning company that's trusted with multi-million-dollar homes. Now I'm more intrigued.

"I'm sure this is a good gig for her."

"Yeah, but what I'm saying is that Kent approves of her. And Kent rarely approves of anyone."

I bite the inside of my cheek. "I should ask her when she's getting there." Nervously, I walk back toward the entryway.

Looking around the foyer, I don't see her. Opening the front door, I notice the cars that were there are now gone. *Shit. That's what you get, Patch—hesitating, overthinking. Classic.* But tomorrow, I won't mess it up.

2

Rachel

Saturday, March 15th

"Good morning," I cheerily answer, seeing Emily's name shine across my phone screen as I get ready for High Five's St. Patrick's Day party.

"Exactly how much green are you wearing?" she asks with a high level of stress in her tone.

"I'm wearing green jeans and a white shirt that says, 'Here for the Paddy.'" *I hope the husky hottie from yesterday makes an appearance.* "Plus," I refocus, "I'm currently in the process of applying a shamrock tattoo on my temple."

"Okay," Emily breathes. My answer seems to lower her stress. "Do you have extra tattoos?" she asks playfully.

"Yeah, tons."

"Bring those to the bar! Nicholas will find it so funny if I wear a bunch."

The happiness in her tone brings a smile to my face. I'm happy for her. She's so smitten with Nicholas, and I love them together.

"Because you don't have tattoos, and he has that epic sleeve?"

"Something like that."

"I'm happy you're getting some again," I joke, hearing the flirtatiousness in her last response. "You're easier to be around."

It's been so long since I felt that comfortable with someone. I miss that—the giddiness, the teasing looks across the room. But instead, I'm the single friend now. *How fucking bizarre!*

"So, you know how my team is cleaning the Dubois house?" I ask, wanting to tell her about the guy from yesterday.

"Your biggest account. How could I forget?"

"I was there yesterday on a last-minute clean, and the owner's son and a friend arrived. They're our age, maybe younger, which was surprising. I always assumed the family was way older. Anyways—off track—I know. The friend," I purr. "He's, like, my perfect dream ... green eyes, husky, bearded ... rawr."

"Rawr?" Emily laughs. "So, you're in love. Got it. Did you make a move?"

"Sort of ... I mentioned that they should come by High Five today."

"Trifecta!" she screams, and I pull the phone away from my ear to save my hearing. "Make it a three-peat!"

"Em, please stop using sports references. It's freaking me out."

"I know." She giggles. "Who would have ever thought I would watch sports with a guy?"

"Not me." I laugh.

"Well, I hope this green-eyed hottie comes by so someone can get lucky!"

Shaking my head, I can't hold back a smirk.

"I'm still getting used to being the only single one in the friend group. It's weird ..." I trail off, thinking about how not long ago, I was the only one regularly dating, and now I'm the only one in a sexual drought.

My New Year's resolution was to stay off the dating apps. They suck, and I'd only been matching with guys looking for a fun night.

Looking at myself in the mirror, I hope he comes by. He's probably from Chicago and not looking for something serious. That's my type, after all, emotionally unavailable pricks ... with huge dicks. One night wouldn't be the worst thing to happen. I would like to know more about the guy besides being very attracted to him, but I want more from guys than that. I'm thirty-one and want something deep, like what my friends have going on.

"See you when the doors open?" I ask, refocusing on my call with Emily.

"You know it!"

3

Patrick

Working out in the Dubois lake house gym is like working out at the most exclusive high-end private gym in the city. It's perfect and has every piece of equipment imaginable. Between squat sets, I search "High Five Lake Geneva," curious to know more about the place.

Fifty-thousand followers! I'm surprised that a bar in a small town is internet famous. I begin watching their TikTok videos. The most recent ones are all about their St. Paddy's party. The doors open at 11:00 a.m. *That's in a couple of hours.* I chew on my lower lip, already debating whether to go.

I'd really like to talk with her ...

She did invite us, but maybe she was just being polite. Showing up alone ... would that seem too forward? Maybe she'd think I'm weird. Or desperate.

Deciding to end my workout with a cardio blast, I step onto the manual treadmill. Running for thirty-seconds, then resting for fifteen, I repeat that a few times before I'm panting and dripping sweat. Examining my body through the mirrored wall, I wonder if maybe I've been too hard on myself. The pump from this session is making me feel a little more confident. Maybe I can pull this off.

No pressure. Just go, talk to her. If the vibe isn't right, I'll head back. No big deal.

After a shower, I empty out my backpack onto the bed in the guest room I picked out. There were so many to choose from, but I like that this bedroom has near panoramic views of Geneva Lake. I hadn't exactly planned on celebrating St. Patrick's Day, and my wardrobe reflects that. A pile of clothes stares back at me—none remotely festive. A white t-shirt and jeans seem like the best option, so I throw them on with a denim jacket. I glance down at the plain white tee and scrunch my nose. Should I stop by a store for something green?

I check High Five's social media again, scrolling through their posts. They're promising an authentic Irish experience with communal games and live music. I don't think actual Irish people go all out with green, right? A quick Google search doesn't clear things up. One article says it's a myth; another has leprechauns plastered all over it. I groan and give up the search, deciding against buying a one-time-use shirt.

Replaying our interaction, why am I assuming she won't be there with someone else? She said she would be there with her friends. If she had a boyfriend, she would've mentioned it, right? *Right?!* The anxiety twists tighter in my chest. What if I show up and she's with someone else? Or worse—what if she doesn't even remember me?

Why am I so fucking anxious? I know the answer before I finish asking the question. Because she's exactly what I'd describe as my dream woman, *that's why.*

I push the thought away as I head downstairs, searching for Brandon. This house is huge—like, absurdly huge—forty rooms, easy. I finally find him in what I think people call a "sitting room." He's lounging on a leather chair, reading some motivational book. The room has a cozy, tucked-away feel, like a miniature library.

"The St. Paddy's thing starts soon. I'm thinking about heading over. You sure you don't want to come with me?"

"Very." Brandon laughs softly, not even looking up from his book.

"I think I'm going to swing by for a beer and then come back."

"Dude, don't rush back because of me," Brandon says, finally glancing up with a smirk. "I didn't expect us to hang out the entire time. Go, have fun."

"You sure you're cool with it?"

"Of course. See where the day takes you," he encourages, closing his book. "Oh, and use the car service. Let me call them."

"Car service?" I raise an eyebrow. "Can't I just Uber?"

"Uber?" He shakes his head. "Not out here, Patch. Especially not in the off-season. Here's this local guy—he's cool. We always use him to drive us around. Trust me. Let me call him."

4

Rachel

"Let's get a few things straight," I announce, leaning forward at our unofficially official table at High Five. "I am not, under any circumstances, going to fuck a leprechaun."

The girls burst into laughter, nearly spitting out their drinks.

"Who's asking you to?" Emily gasps, still laughing, her drink sloshing dangerously close to the table's edge.

"You got Santa," I remind her, smirking. "Sarah got Cupid. And next up is a leprechaun, which is a firm no from me."

"What if he has a pot of gold?" Emily teases, raising an eyebrow.

"Or can grant three wishes," Sarah adds, her chuckle joining Emily's.

I shake my head, deadpan. "Not even if he could give me a billion wishes and a private island."

Sarah leans in, smirking. "Well, a short king would still be tall compared to you."

"This short girl likes tall guys," I remind them, giving Sarah a playful nudge.

My eyes scan the bar hoping Mr. Rawr—definitely not a short king or a leprechaun—makes an appearance. Green streamers and shamrocks decorate the ceiling and walls, making the place look as cheesy and festive as always for these themed events. Not as over-the-top as the last couple of holiday pop-ups, but still enough to remind you it's St. Paddy's. The music's loud, the drinks are flowing, and Mr. Rawr is on my mind.

"Look at her," Emily says. "When was the last time she looked this excited?"

"Catch a girl up!" Sarah says, noticing the shift in my body language.

"There's this guy," I say, unable to suppress a smile. "I asked him to come here. He's staying at the Dubois house."

Sarah lets out a mock gasp. "Big money ... a pot of gold! That's a St. Patrick's Day reference!" She cracks herself up, clearly pleased with the connection.

While I'm laughing with her, my eyes are again on the door.

Was I being too obvious yesterday? Probably. Mr. Rawr is worth it. He's hot, but there's something else too. The way he looked at me ... it wasn't just the typical *hey, you're hot* glance. There was this uncertainty, this mix of fear and interest, like he was both scared shitless and intrigued all at once. It was cute, in a shy, quiet sort of way. I love nerds, not that I go for them as much as I should though.

Emily nudges me, breaking through my thoughts. "You never get this worked up over guys."

"Worked up?" I squint then wave a hand dismissively. "Please, I'm as cool as a cucumber."

Sarah shoots me a skeptical look, eyebrow raised. "Sure,

that's why you've been checking the door every five seconds."

I squint at both of them, unwilling to give in to their teasing. They know me too well, but that doesn't mean I'm going to let on how much I want him to show up. My heart rate elevates when I think about seeing him again, but I play it cool, sipping my drink.

Our favorite bartender and Sarah's new boyfriend, Aaron, slides over to our table. He sets a pitcher of water down in front of us. "Remember, ladies, today is a marathon, not a sprint."

We all laugh, but as soon as Aaron walks off, I see *him*. I loudly inhale, my breath catching. There he is—Mr. Rawr—walking through the door like a damn dream.

5

Patrick

I stare at the hole-in-the-wall bar in front of me, my heartbeat already outpacing my breath. *What the hell am I doing here?* My anxiety spikes, and I find myself second-guessing every decision that led me here. What if she isn't here yet? St. Paddy's is more of a day-drinking holiday ... I hope my assumption is correct that she would be here now. Tugging at the collar of my denim jacket, I'm suddenly aware that I'm underdressed with not a hint of green in sight. *Idiot.*

I swallow hard and step inside. The scent of old wood and beer smacks me in the face. It's busier than I expected. Was coming here a mistake? People are already crammed into corners, pint glasses clinking as they celebrate. I scan the room, trying to blend into the shadows when—

There she is.

Sitting with two other girls, laughing easily, completely at ease. She's so beautiful, her energy filling the space around her, while I feel like an outsider. My palms are damp. *Why did I think I could do this?* My legs are locked in place, but I force myself to move. I've come this far—I can't back out now. I take a deep breath and start walking toward her, my heart beating so fast. It feels faster than it did in my workout this morning.

She looks amazing, leaning back at the table like she owns the place. Confidence just radiates off her. Brown hair, blue eyes, and a perfect face. She's wearing a shirt that says "Here for the Paddy," with green jeans and white sneakers. She looks effortlessly cool—*way* out of my league. My mind screams at me to turn around, but instead, I open my mouth.

"Hey." *I said that too loud.* It's loud in here. Before I can overthink my volume, my eyes lock on a tiny shamrock tattoo near her temple. *Why is that so cute?* My brain stumbles over itself. I have to remind myself to inhale.

"You made it!" She seems surprised ... in a good way. Her blue eyes are brighter than I expected. Like she's excited to see me. *Wait, what?*

When I reach the table, I go for the handshake, which feels wrong the second I extend my hand. "I'm Patrick."

The other two girls burst out laughing, and I feel my cheeks heat up. Was it weird to shake her hand? God, why did I do that? But then she firmly shakes it with a smile.

"I'm Rachel." I notice a bit of blush on her cheek. Maybe there's some inside joke I'm not aware of instead of the alternative—that they're laughing at me for shaking her hand. "And this is Emily and Sarah." She points at her friends. Emily's wearing a t-shirt that says "Lucky," and Sarah's t-shirt reads "Cheers, Bitches."

"Where's your friend?" Rachel asks.

I hesitate, deflated. Of course she'd be interested in wealthy, stereotypically attractive Brandon. "He's sitting this one out."

"Too cool for a townie bar?" She raises an eyebrow, and

with that tone in her voice, relief washes over me. Maybe I was wrong.

"No, uh ... he's sober."

"Ah," Rachel says, and the mood shifts before Emily jumps in. "Where's your green?" she asks.

"I wasn't planning on celebrating the holiday."

"Patrick doesn't go all in on St. Patrick's Day?" Rachel teases.

"I'm not much of a partier," I respond, more sheepish than I'd like.

"Neither are we," she replies quickly, flashing a smile that catches me by surprise. *Maybe I still have a shot here.*

I take a breath, gathering what little courage I have left. "Can I buy you and your friends a round of drinks?"

"My friends are already drinking for free." The other two giggle. "Emily is dating the guy that owns the place, Nicholas," she explains, pointing at a guy behind the bar wearing a white and green White Sox jersey with an impressive Celtic sleeve tattoo. "And Sarah is dating that guy—Aaron." She points at the other tall guy behind the bar wearing a green tank top that says, "Whiskey Helps."

Well, there goes that plan. I hesitate, feeling my options slip away. "Can I buy *you* a drink?"

"Yeah. An Irish coffee, please."

I smile, nodding. I'm starting to think this wasn't a bad idea after all.

"That sounds good. I think I'll get one to," I say, trying to play it cool as I head for the bar. My nerves are still there, but now they're a little more manageable. *Maybe I can actually pull this off.*

6

Rachel

"Rachel!" Sarah squeals as Patrick walks toward the bar. "His name is *Patrick*! Are you *fucking* kidding me?!"

"There's something magical about this place," Emily chimes in, amused. "And you know you drink for free, right?"

"I know, but I wasn't going to tell him that."

We exchange glances, an almost electric energy buzzing between us.

"Don't get ahead of yourselves," I warn, though I can't hide my own excitement. "I'm barely keeping my cool as it is ... because *look* at that guy."

"If that's not your future husband, I don't know who is," Emily teases.

"I know! I'm freaking out right now!" My heart is racing. He's exactly my type. And his eyes without the glasses ... holy shit. They are so green.

"Seriously," Sarah adds, biting her lip to stifle her laughter. "I'm already picking out bridesmaid dresses."

"Stop," I hiss, though I can't hold back a smile. Aaron

notices how we're all staring at Patrick and winks at us as he finishes making the Irish coffees.

"Be cool, *please*," I whisper, panic rising slightly as Patrick heads back.

He returns with the drinks and a damp cloth in hand, his expression confused, like he's trying to decode some sort of puzzle. His eyebrows knit together, and I find him so cute.

"Aaron, right?" he asks as he sets the drinks down. We all nod.

"He said we needed this?" Patrick places the cloth in the center of the table. I smile, thoroughly impressed that Aaron's playing wingman.

As Patrick takes a seat, his knee bumps into mine, and the simple contact sends my heart rate back up. I try not to react, but my body betrays me as my cheeks flush again. He's so close. I check him out, noticing how his jacket stretches over his broad shoulders. *Patrick's strong.*

"If you're going to sit with us, you need to be initiated," Sarah says, ever the instigator.

Patrick raises an eyebrow. "Should I be scared? Am I joining the cult of cute brunettes?"

We all laugh. I hadn't thought about how my best friends and I are all brunettes before, and how he, Nicholas, and Aaron are also brunettes.

"Looks that way." His green eyes are unlike anything I've ever seen. I could stare at them for hours, but I break our eye contact, taking a sip of my drink.

"Pick a tattoo," Emily says, sliding a pile of temporary tattoos his way.

He laughs softly, sorting through the pile with a thoughtful expression, deciding on a shamrock that matches mine. "Where should I put it?" he asks, his voice dropping just a little as his eyes land on mine.

Oh. I take my time, letting my eyes wander over his body, his neck, his jawline, dragging out the decision. *This guy is so fucking hot.* I don't think he's beard fishing. I think he would be just as hot without the beard. But I like beard. Patrick is exactly my type—the kind who lifts weights and also eats carbs.

I lean in, tapping the skin on his neck. "Right here."

"Rachel, do the honors," Emily encourages.

Best friends ever. I peel back the plastic, and as I place the tattoo on his neck, I press the damp cloth against his skin. The air between us thickens, and I feel my heart pounding in my chest. His eyes hold mine, charged with a quiet intensity. The longer I hold the cloth, the more I feel the heat building between us.

Taking a peek, I smile. "All set."

"So, Patrick," Sarah starts. "What should we know about you? What does your Hinge bio say?"

He nervously laughs, shaking his head. "I'm off the apps."

"Same," I add quickly. "The apps are a dumpster fire."

He smiles at me, then takes a sip of his drink. "I'm twenty-seven—"

Emily doesn't miss a beat. "What do you think about dating an older woman?"

He narrows his eyes, amused. "Aren't we the same age?"

"We're all thirty-one," I say, holding his gaze a little longer than I mean to. "Well, Emily's almost thirty-one."

He bites his lip, and something flickers behind his eyes—something playful but also curious.

"What?" I prod.

"Age is just a number." The way he looks at me when

he says it ... I know I'm blushing again. I try to stay composed, but I can feel my pulse quicken. *He's smooth, but it feels real.* "I guess you should know that I work in cybersecurity, live in the Wicker Park neighborhood of Chicago, and grew up on a farm in Minnesota."

"Farm to cybersecurity? That's random."

He nods, his expression softening. "Yeah, my parents still don't really understand what I do."

We all laugh, but there's something in his tone that's disarming. There's a vulnerability there—a kind of "nice guy" energy that feels real, like he's still nervous talking to the three of us. It's kind of sweet. No, scratch that—it's really sweet.

"Attention, High Fivers," a voice crackles over the speaker. "It's almost time for our beer pong tournament. Sign-up closes in five minutes."

Patrick raises an eyebrow at me, wordlessly asking, *Should we?*

"Are you any good?"

"No."

I laugh, appreciating his honesty. "Well, same."

"Let's be the worst team then," he suggests before taking a sip of his Irish coffee.

I nod, smiling. "Last place champs. I'm in."

7

Patrick

"We have to finish a pint—just one between the two of us—before the game is over," I say, reviewing the laminated rule sheet. "And the cups are only filled with water. No drinking out of the cups."

"Easy enough." Rachel glances up at me, smiling. She barely reaches my shoulder, the perfect height difference. My nerves have calmed a bit, and I'm starting to relax more.

"How long have your friends been dating those guys?" I ask, nodding toward the high-boy table where her friends are sitting with their boyfriends.

"Both are pretty new. Nicholas and Emily made it official about two months ago, and Sarah and Aaron have been together for about a month."

"Is your ex named Patrick or something?" I'm still curious about the way her friends reacted earlier.

She laughs, shaking her head. "No."

"Then why did they giggle so much when I introduced myself?" *I hope it wasn't my awkward handshake.*

She smiles, her eyes teasing. "Tell you what—if we win this game, I'll tell you."

"I thought we were aiming for last-place champs?"

"Maybe I changed my mind." Rachel shrugs mischievously.

Well, now I'm motivated.

"Hey," I say, changing the subject. "I saw you wearing earbuds yesterday. I could never—how are they comfortable for you?"

"They just are?"

"I'm a big headphones guy."

"Fits with your hot, nerdy vibe."

She thinks I'm hot?! I blink, thrown off.

"So, are you a New Balance or Nike kind of guy?" she asks, checking me out with a playful look.

She's flirting with me?! There is no need to overanalyze this. I was telling myself she was being nice before, but this is blatant flirting. "What do you think?" I flirt back.

"New Balance seems obvious, but maybe you're a sneakerhead." She gives me a quick once-over, looking down at my shoes. "Or maybe you don't wear mainstream brands."

"I own, like, five pairs of shoes. I'm trying to be a minimalist."

"Well, I own about a hundred pairs, so I'm not sure this will work."

I take a sip of the beer to gather myself, unable to say what I'm thinking, which is that it wouldn't be a deal breaker. *I'm so flustered.*

"I saw you wearing glasses yesterday. How blind are you?" She's clearly enjoying this game of back and forth or enjoying how fucking nervous she's making me.

"I don't know what the definition of legally blind is, but I have to be close."

"Same. I couldn't function without contacts or glasses."

"I promise my eyes are worse."

"Well, one of us should always carry glasses then," she jokes. "For safety."

"For safety." Even though I might have a heart attack, I like this rhythm between us.

"You're really bad," she says as I miss again.

Our opponents are pros, and they're demolishing us. The balls keep sinking into our cups with painful precision.

"I wasn't much of a party guy in college. More of a gamer, hacker kinda guy."

"Hacking?"

"Yeah." I don't want to bore her, but she looks interested. "I hacked into the company I work for now. Caused enough of an inconvenience that they hired me."

"Badass!"

She thinks that's cool? That makes me feel more confident.

Meanwhile, our opponents—a couple of early-twenties guys—are getting smug, landing another ball with ease. Rachel's face scrunches up in frustration.

"It's kind of a common story for hackers," I continue, trying to keep the conversation going. "Unless they're 'black hat,' which means they're motivated by chaos or money."

"Black hat?"

"Yeah, there are three types: black, gray, and white. White hats are the good guys. Black hats are the bad ones. Gray hats ... well, we're somewhere in between."

"*We're*," she repeats, narrowing her eyes at me playfully. "I like morally gray guys."

"What's that supposed to mean?"

"Nothing." She giggles, and I squint at her, not fully understanding the joke, but I'm loving the banter.

The other team rolls the ping pong balls back to us. Rachel grabs both and hands one to me. Without thinking, I take her hand in mine and kiss it. "For good luck," I say, surprised with myself by the bold gesture.

Her face lights up. "I don't want to lose to these guys," she whispers, her expression suddenly serious as she concentrates on the game. She tosses the ball, and it lands perfectly in the cup.

"Yeah!" I shout, high-fiving her.

Now it's my turn. The pressure is on, and I know I need to make this. Taking a deep breath, I aim and toss the ball.

"You made one!"

"All luck, no skill." I wink.

"You've got one more shot to prove luck is on your side."

The guys roll the balls back to us, and Rachel scoops them up.

"If we both make it again, we could be back in this." She extends her hand to me. "Kiss it—for good luck."

I smirk, covering her hand with mine and kissing her knuckle. We hold a flirty stare until I break away and take a sip of the beer, which we haven't even touched yet.

"You got this," I say, chuckling at how focused she is on the game now.

Rachel takes a deep breath, holding the ball at shoulder level. With a flick of her wrist, it lands in a cup again.

"You're on fire!" She's jumping in excitement, being too cute.

Now the pressure is *really* on. I have to make this. *Please, go into the cup,* I internally tell the ball as I toss it.

"You're heating up!" she cheers when it goes in, and without warning, she playfully smacks my ass. I turn to look at her in surprise, and she does this shrug-shimmy thing that makes me smile.

"Double bring-backs!" one of the guys shouts, impressed by our comeback.

Rachel smiles, putting the balls back in her hand. "For good luck?" she asks, teasingly extending them toward me.

Wrapping my hand around hers, I guess we're leaning into superstition, and I kiss the same knuckle again. "For good luck."

The tension between us is thick. There's a new competitiveness and something more. Rachel flicks her wrist, and we both watch in slow motion as the ball hits the cup—then bounces off the rim.

She groans, her face deflating in the most adorable way. I pull her into a side hug, trying to cheer her up. "Two in a row was impressive," I say, my arm still around her shoulders.

"Give me the beer. I'm mad."

I laugh, handing her the glass. I love how into the game she's getting. It's hot.

"If I make the next one ..." I pause, gauging if I should say what I'm thinking. I take a sip of the beer, deciding if I'm really going to say this. The vibes are definitely there ... "*If* I make it ... I get to smack your ass."

She devilishly laughs, extending her hand to take the beer from me. After a long sip, she looks up at me. "If you make this, I'll kiss you."

Whoa. Her words hang between us, and I've never been

more motivated in my life. I look into her eyes, then down at her lips, and back up again.

I take a deep breath to focus. *I have to make this.*

8

Rachel

Staring at Patrick, I really want him to make this. It's the perfect excuse to kiss him. I know we just met, but who cares? I want it.

His brows furrow slightly, like he's putting everything he has into this shot. He's so nervous. It's cute—more than cute, actually. Then, suddenly, the Irish music from the speakers stops, and the change in sound catches both of us off guard. We glance toward the DJ booth, now replaced by a four-member band starting their sound check. The moment feels suspended, like everything is waiting for something to happen.

"You got this," I whisper. He smiles back at me, and I am seriously crushing on this guy.

Patrick tosses the ball. *Land in the cup!* I'm praying like I've never prayed before. It feels like the entire room holds its breath with me.

But it misses.

"Airball," the guys across the table taunt, but their voices barely register.

I grab his shirt, pulling him down to me, and our lips

crash together. It's tentative at first but then his hand cups my face, and everything changes. The noise around us blurs as the kiss deepens. I feel on fire as his tongue meets mine, and I don't want this to end.

"But I didn't make it," he whispers, pulling back slightly.

"I still wanted to kiss you."

He presses his forehead firmly against mine, and a swirl of emotions floods through me. It's so tender. Too cute. This kiss. It's the beginning of something, and suddenly, I want more. So much more.

The rest of the game passes in a blur. Neither of us is really paying attention. Our hands can't seem to stay off each other, fingers laced together, soft kisses pressed to knuckles before each shot. We laugh as we try to Irish jig to the music when it's not our turn, both of us stumbling awkwardly but not caring.

I should feel tipsy from the Irish coffee and the beer, but it's not the alcohol making my head spin—it's him. It's the way we're completely caught up in each other, the way Patrick's touch sends little sparks through me every time his hand brushes mine. I'm drunk on this flirtation, on the way we keep finding excuses to be closer, and I don't want it to end. For once, I'm not thinking ahead, not worrying about what comes next. I'm just here, with him.

"Last place champs!" I high-five Patrick when we officially lose the game. The smack of our hands echoes, but then his fingers slide between mine, pulling me toward him for another kiss. Our lips collide, softer this time, but it's no less intoxicating.

"I'd say I won."

I smile into another kiss, feeling my heart swell.

"Lovebirds." Nicholas's voice pops our little bubble. "Lunch was dropped at your table."

As we walk back, hand in hand, I can't stop thinking about how much I'm liking this guy, how natural this is between us. We barely know each other, but it feels like there's something real here, something so different from the dumpster fire the apps have brought me.

9

Patrick

"I'm having so much fun with you," I say after taking a bite of the cheesy fries, unable to hold back the smile glued to my face. She's forward, and I like that. I can't believe she kissed me. "Do you want another drink or ..."

Or? What am I even asking? It's not even 1:00 p.m. Am I seriously suggesting that she come back with me already? I can feel the heat rise to my face, regretting the words as soon as they're out of my mouth.

"A Guinness please." She smiles, saving me from my own awkwardness. Her eyes flick toward the tattoo pile. "When you come back, you're getting another one."

I nod and head toward the bar, feeling a weird mixture of relief and nervousness. Standing there, waiting for Aaron to notice me, I can't shake the feeling that I'm being watched. I glance around and spot Nicholas making his way over. He's older than the girls and Aaron, closer to forty.

"I'm Patrick." I extend my hand, and he shakes it, but there's something off in his expression—like he's sizing me up.

"How do you know Rachel?"

"We met ... yesterday."

"You live in the city?" he asks, but it's less of a question and more of a statement. He already knows, and I guess information between the friends travels fast.

"Yeah."

Nicholas's face shifts slightly, like he's already made up his mind about me. It's subtle, but I catch the flicker of judgment. Maybe he thinks we're moving too fast—he saw how flirty we were. I can't believe we were kissing either. That's never happened for me ... randomly kissing a girl I just met.

"Rachel isn't just some story for you to tell your friends about on Monday," Nicholas says, and I hear the warning in his voice.

My chest tightens, but before I can respond, Aaron breaks the tension, "What can I get you?"

"Two Guinnesses." My voice is steady, but my mind is racing. *I'm not that guy.*

"Comp them," Nicholas says with a nod to Aaron, then walks away without another word. I'm left standing there, beers in hand, unsure of how to process that interaction.

"He's protective," Aaron says, sliding the beers across the bar to me. "We just want the girls to have a good time, but Chicago guys don't have the best reputation here."

"What's that supposed to mean?"

"Lots of girls come in here, meet a guy who's just in town for the weekend, and end up heartbroken when he doesn't call back." Aaron pauses, his eyes meeting mine. "We see it happen a lot."

"I'm not that guy," I state firmly, gripping the beers a little tighter. I don't think this is the time to share my lack of dating history and extremely small body count. Turning on my heels, I head back to Rachel.

"I think you need this one," Rachel says, holding up a

laughing leprechaun tattoo as I set the beers down in front of her.

"Does that mean I get to pick one out for you?" I ask, although the guys' warnings are replaying in my head.

She nods, and I rummage through the pile, finding a pair of green lips. I hold it up with a raised brow.

"Fun!"

As I press the cloth into her neck, I manage, "So, where do you live?"

"Here, in Lake Geneva. Born and raised."

"Her house is so cute," Sarah chimes in from the side, and I smirk a little. Should I read that as a subtle invitation to see her place? *At least the girls like me.*

"It's small, but it's mine," Rachel adds.

"You own it?" I ask, impressed.

"Yeah, I bought it a couple of years ago."

This detail makes her even more attractive, and suddenly, the idea of cuddling up at her house feels like the perfect ending to this day. But there's a part of me that holds back. *Is this too fast?*

"I'm feeling lucky," Rachel says, and I sip my beer, stuffing down the potential innuendo. "Ever played pull tabs?"

"Of course. It's like no-tech slots. Do they have them here?" I look around for the machine that dispenses the paper gambling cards.

"Yes! We should play!" Her excitement is infectious.

I pull out my wallet and take out a twenty-dollar bill, holding it out to her. "Here, let's see if we can win big."

"Big spender." Rachel winks.

I shrug. "Better odds this way."

She takes the twenty and slides off the tall chair. As she

walks past, she gives me a playful poke in the side, and I feel a rush of excitement.

"Twenty pull tabs," she says as she returns, handing out a few to Emily, Sarah, me, and keeping some for herself. "Top prize is five hundred dollars."

Rachel cracks the side of the cardboard and pulls all of the tabs on her card at once.

"You're a savage," I tease, surprised she didn't savor it.

"Not a winner." She giggles, shrugging.

"I like to take my time," I say, pulling each tab slowly. She winks, and I can't help but smirk.

"Fifty dollars!" Rachel squeals.

"No way!"

She waves the winning card to me, and sure enough—fifty bucks. I finish pulling the tabs on my last one and chuckle. "One dollar."

"You're a winner too!"

"So, do we cash these in or roll the winnings into more pull tabs?"

"Are you serious?! You doubled your money—cash out."

"There's still a five-hundred-dollar winner in there. We could have fifty-one more chances to get it."

"It's too risky."

I run my hand through my beard, enjoying this new insight into her risk tolerance. "Whatever you want. But if it were just up to me, I'd go big."

"I don't want us to be big losers. Right now, we're winning."

We exchange smiles. "I've never really explored Lake Geneva before," I share, taking another sip of my beer.

I'm trying to focus on her and how easy everything feels, but Nicholas's words linger. I don't want to feel like I have something to prove—but I do.

10

Rachel

Patrick has been such a good sport, hanging out with my friends, laughing at their jokes, even fitting in like he's known them for more than a few hours. As much fun as this is, I want to get to know him without other people around.

"How about I give you a tour of Main Street after this beer?"

He smiles. "I'd love that."

We hold a flirty gaze, and I ask him, "Tell me more about some gray hacking you've done."

He bites his lip before sipping his beer. "I once redirected a politician's website to a gay porn site."

The girls and I all laugh.

"It feels like you have more stories like this," Emily encourages.

"I have a lot of stories like this ..." He trails off, and I see the assuredness. He's not showing off—he's just *him,* and I'm being drawn in by every word.

"Tell us!" I demand.

"In college, my friends and I would do something every weekend."

"Stop being coy." I playfully swat his arm. "He told me he hacked the company he works for and that's how he got his job," I share with the girls.

"So, Patrick is cute and clever." Sarah smiles. "What else should we know about you?"

"I'm getting into powerlifting," he says and my friends exchange glances that don't go unnoticed by me. Yeah, I know—guys that lift, another box he's checking.

"What can you deadlift?" I ask, curious and also challenging.

"At least two of you."

My cheeks flush and my mind drifts, imagining him easily picking me up, and I take another sip of my beer to cool myself down. Although he can pick me up and throw me around any time he wants. *Chill.*

"Have you ever heard of the F.I.R.E. concept?" he asks.

My friends and I all shake our heads.

"It stands for 'Financially Independent, Retire Early.' I'm hoping to retire by forty, and I'm pretty nerdy about investing."

Sarah and Emily both look impressed, and I feel my interest rise another notch. *He's twenty-seven and already planning his future like this?*

"I own about five shares of Disney stock that I got from my grandparents when I was a kid. That's all I know about the market," I admit.

"I can bore you about it anytime you want."

I laugh, but my mind is spinning. *How is he twenty-seven and this mature?* He's checking every box, and I'm not sure what to do with that.

We finish our beers, and I glance at his empty glass,

feeling the moment hovering between us. "Ready for a tour?" I ask, and he nods.

As I slide into my jacket, I catch him checking me out, and a smug smile creeps across my face. I lean in closer, teasing, "Stop checking me out."

"Why?"

My heart skips a beat. *Fuck.* I might actually sleep with him—not right now, but later ... if this keeps progressing the way it's been. I want to, but I shouldn't. I barely know him. *But damn, I want to.*

I shake off the thought as I turn to hug Emily. "See you later," I say, and then I move to hug Sarah, who pulls me in close.

"We do not want to see you later," she whispers in my ear, making me giggle.

"It's not going to be that long of a tour," I share as Patrick and I step outside. "Main Street isn't that big."

11

Patrick

Outside of the bar, I contemplate grabbing her hand. *I mean, we did kiss.* But before I can make a move, she reaches for my hand first. The simple gesture makes me smile, and I squeeze her hand, interlacing our fingers. *So easy. So natural.*

"Rachel," I say, breaking the quiet. "What's your last name?"

"Wagner. What's yours?"

"Nowak."

She flashes a smile, then points to a nearby shop. "This is a cute place where you can buy everything your grandma could ever want."

What a spot-on description, I think, looking at the window display.

"And this," she points to another store, "is where you can find the stupidest t-shirts you'll ever see."

I nod in agreement, reading some of the shirts in the window.

"Should we get one?" she asks eagerly. "Like stupid matching ones?"

It's a cute idea, but I share, "I'm in a minimalist phase."

"How hardcore minimalist are we talking?"

"Not too extreme. I'm just trying not to buy stuff for the sake of buying stuff."

"I feel that, but sometimes you have to make an impulse purchase like the temporary tattoos."

I smile, leaning down to kiss the little tattoo on her temple. "I'm glad you bought them."

She looks up at me, a little sparkle in her eyes. "You're pretty smooth, you know?"

"I don't know about that."

"You don't think so?"

I lower my voice and lean in close, almost whispering. "I'm so nervous talking with you."

"What?" She stops, standing in place on the sidewalk. "Why?"

I bite my lip, holding her gaze a little longer than necessary before answering. "You're the prettiest girl I've ever kissed."

Her cheeks flush, and she twirls a piece of her brown hair with her free hand. "Well ... you look like the mood board of my dream man."

Did she really just say that? I stop walking, tugging her gently toward me for a kiss. This one isn't as tentative as before. It's slower, deeper—full of the feeling that I can't believe this is happening either. There's something about this kiss that says more than words. *This connection is real.*

When we pull away, her smile is bright, and she points to a nearby shop. "Sarah owns that one. It's a maker's studio."

"That's amazing. Are you all small business owners?"

"Not Emily. She has a six-year-old and does marketing for a law firm in town."

Walking, holding hands, I feel so content and realize I haven't looked at my phone since I got to the bar. Digital detox. It's going well, and Rachel is more interesting than anything on my phone.

"It's kind of freaking me out that this is happening," Rachel says into the silence.

"What do you mean?"

"High Five ... it's like it has this magic or something." She pauses, glancing back at the bar. "It's how Emily and Nicholas got together. It's how Sarah and Aaron started flirting. And now ..." She trails off but keeps looking up at me.

I smirk, leaning in a little closer. "But we met at the Dubois house."

"Well, you didn't kiss me there ..."

"I could ..."

Did I really just say that? It came out before I could stop myself, but it's how I feel.

"Yeah right. I'm not hooking up there. It's my biggest client, and I can't mess that up."

So, she's not opposed to hooking up, just ... not there. I bite my lip, trying to push down how overwhelmed I feel that she could be thinking about me in that way.

"I haven't felt like this in forever," Rachel says softly.

"What do you mean?"

She hesitates. "I'm probably going to freak you out, but I was engaged before. To my high school sweetheart."

I know plenty of people who've been in that situation. *Small towns.*

"We almost got married, but I called it off. I felt like ... I felt like he had his whole life mapped out, and at first, I liked that. But eventually, I realized I didn't know who I was yet, and I didn't want to get married when I wasn't even sure what

I wanted for myself." She looks up at me, her eyes soft but serious. "I didn't go to college. I've worked every kind of job around here and started a cleaning company a few years ago."

"Running your own business is no joke," I say, admiring her even more now. "And if you're managing places like the Dubois house, you're doing something right."

She smiles, and I can't get over how beautiful she is. Of course she's gorgeous but ... her energy, her warmth.

"I can relate, actually," I share. "I've always been into computers, but I wasn't sure how I wanted to spend my time until I got the job I have now. Hacking has always been fun, but this job—it's like the pieces of my life finally started to fit."

"That's how I feel now too, like the pieces have finally come together."

"Most of them," I say, gently nudging her.

She tilts her head, raising an eyebrow. "Most?"

"Well ... I'd love to have someone to share it all with."

"Same."

We smile at each other, and it feels like the conversation just shifted into something deeper, something neither of us wants to say out loud just yet.

"So, this F.I.R.E. thing," she says, changing the subject. "I bet it helps that you probably make a lot of money in cybersecurity."

"I've made more money hacking."

"I thought you said you were gray, not black."

"There are companies out there that offer rewards or prizes for hacking them. It's a way to test their security. I've made more money from that than my actual job."

Her eyes narrow playfully before she says, "It's kind of hot that you're a hacker."

"Not as hot as you in a *Brand New* crop top."

She smirks, squeezing my hand as we continue to slowly walk along Main Street. "Do you know that band?"

"Know them? It's taking everything in me not to say one of their most famous lyrics to you."

"Hopefully it's not 'die young and save yourself.'" She nudges her shoulder into me.

"I'm thinking of one of their other depressing songs ... that is also kind of romantic."

"Aren't you a little young to be into emo music?" she teasingly asks me.

"I thought emo music was more related to being fucked up than age."

She laughs deeply before saying, "Fair." Shaking her head, she then looks up at me. "Why are you fucked up?"

"How much time do we have?"

"Don't tease me, Patrick."

Rachel saying my name. *Fuck.*

"Maybe after I take you out on a date, we can talk about that."

"See!" She swats my arm. "You have game. Stop telling me you don't."

"I'm just happy you don't find me boring."

"How could I?"

"Plenty of people do."

She shakes her head. "Not me." Her smile widens, and I can't resist anymore.

"Come here," I whisper, pulling her into another kiss. This time, I let my hands slide down to her waist and then squeeze her ass. When we break apart, I tease, "You've got to tell me your workout routine because your ass says you lift too."

She throws her head back laughing, and I smile, watching her. I really like her.

12

Rachel

"I go to the gym a couple of times a week," I say, smiling. "But honestly, cleaning houses is a workout in itself."

"I bet." But then his phone starts ringing with a sound that's vaguely familiar. *It sounds like that video game my brother used to play.* Before I can place it, Patrick's expression shifts.

"Fuck," he mutters, pulling his phone from his pocket. "What's up?" he answers, pausing mid-step on the sidewalk. A male voice comes through the line, speaking rapidly. Patrick's brows furrow.

"They penetrated that?!"

I can't help it—I burst out laughing. He squeezes my hand and glances at me, mouthing "Sorry," while the guy on the phone keeps talking.

After a few seconds, Patrick pulls the phone down and taps the mute button. "I have to head back and get on my laptop for at least an hour ..."

"Oh ..."

"There's a small team trying to steal someone's Bitcoin

from our platform. It's kind of an all-hands-on-deck situation."

I'm taken aback by the seriousness in his voice. "I can drive you back," I offer.

"You don't have to do that. I'll call a ride."

"No, I'll drive you. I can hang at the house until you're done."

His eyes search mine, unsure. "It might take more than an hour."

"I think you're going to work as fast as you can."

Patrick lets out a breath and smiles. "I will," he says, leaning down to kiss the top of my head. "So, where's your car?"

I nod back toward High Five, and we start walking. "The CEO of the company is on mute right now, so I really need to get back to him."

"Um, casual." I laugh, impressed and more than a little curious. *CEO?* Patrick unmutes the phone, and I hear him say, "I'm actually in Lake Geneva right now. It's going to be a few minutes until I get back to my laptop."

As we walk, I sneak a glance at him and pull out my phone. Cryptoball. I quickly Google it, wanting to know more about the company. *Right.* The CEO is Declan Kruk ... he owns the most expensive house on Geneva Lake. That's why it sounds familiar.

The more I read about the company, the more fascinated I am. This is a *huge* company, and Patrick is talking with the CEO right now.

"The other backdoor," I hear him say, and I giggle again. *Why does everything have a double meaning?*

Patrick squeezes my hand again. "I'm really sorry," he says after hanging up.

"It sounds like it's an urgent situation."

"Our CEO offers five million dollars to anyone who can hack into our systems, so ..." He trails off. I wonder if he's nervous about what he just said.

"So, you're a millionaire, got it," I tease. He did tell me he hacked into this company earlier.

"Not many people know that," he says, definitely more cautious now. "Anyway, this person has hacked enough that they're close to getting that money, but ... it sounds more like a black hat situation."

"They're trying to steal Bitcoin?" I ask, wanting to know more.

He nods, his face serious. "Yes, which would be really, really bad for the company's reputation if they succeed. It's never happened before."

"Should we walk faster?"

Patrick laughs, but the stress is still visible in his eyes. "My team is handling it for now, but when I get back, I need to review everything."

His team? I raise an eyebrow. "I think you've been downplaying your career."

"It's my job ... I don't want a career. I want to be retired, especially when shit like this happens."

He's stressed. We silently walk to my SUV. *We were just starting to connect, and now this?* I feel a little deflated.

"Can I be rude and be on my phone the entire drive back?" he asks, giving my hand a little squeeze.

"Of course. I won't bother you until you're ready for me to bother you."

"You're not bothering me. Work is."

Sitting on the couch overlooking the lake, I realize I've never truly enjoyed this house before. It's always been about work—frantic cleaning sessions with my team, racing against the clock. Even with four people, this place takes hours to get through. But now, sitting here with nothing to do but wait, I take it all in. *It really is beautiful.*

"Hey," a voice interrupts my thoughts. I glance up to see the Dubois guy I met briefly yesterday.

"Hey," I respond, suddenly self-conscious about being here. "Sorry, I'm just waiting for Patrick."

"You're a guest, I know," he says, giving me a casual smile. "Patch told me what's going on. Can I get you anything?"

Patch? That's cute. I smile, feeling more relaxed. "Water would be great."

"Brandon, by the way," he says, handing me the water.

"Rachel."

He leans against the wall, looking thoughtful. "I'm proud of him, you know. For flirting with you. He's usually his own worst enemy when it comes to women."

"Well, I'm happy he showed up today. He's ... cool."

"The coolest."

I'm curious now about their friendship. "How did you two become friends?"

"We work at the same company."

"Are you a hacker too?"

He laughs. "I'm not that smart. I'm more of a relationships guy. I focus on bringing high-net-worth clients to the platform."

Rich kid, makes sense.

"Patrick seems like a big deal at your company," I say, testing the waters.

"He is. CIO."

I cock my head. "CIO?"

"Chief Information Officer."

I blink, his title sinking in. *Why did he downplay this?* "Why didn't he mention that?"

Brandon shrugs. "Because that's just him ..." He hesitates, then smirks. "If you want to learn something epic about Patch, you should Google his name and casino hack 2021."

Now I'm really curious. I pull out my phone again, and when I search, the results make my heart race. *Patrick Nowak.*

"Holy shit," I whisper to myself. *He's like ... a real hacker.* My jaw drops as I read. The casino hack. He and a group of guys took down an entire casino, putting cats on all of the slot machine screens. *Cats.* Funny. He said he wasn't black hat. "Whoa," I breathe out. Felony charges? Computer Fraud and Abuse Act violations? My eyes keep scanning the article until I see the charges were dropped, and the casino later hired him as a consultant.

That was nearly four years ago. Four years ago, he was twenty-three. Four years ago, I was engaged and planning a wedding. Both of us are living such different lives now.

And for some reason, instead of being freaked out, I'm even more intrigued by him. Chuckling to myself, I wonder why I'm so turned on right now.

Patrick rounds the corner, and I look up, still reeling from everything I've learned.

"What's so funny?"

"Your life," I say, shaking my head.

"My life?"

"Brandon gave me some things to research."

Patrick's expression tightens. "Oh ..."

"Good thing you're not a convicted felon."

"You don't want to know how much I've spent on lawyers."

"Seems like it was worth it ..."

"I agree."

We stand there, the severity of everything hanging between us. *What should I do with this information?*

"So ..." I start, trying to gather my thoughts.

"So," Patrick echoes, smiling. "I'm not going to be bothered until Monday morning, and I told Declan he has to hire your company to clean his lake house for the inconvenience. What's your number? I'll text it to him."

"That's how you're going to ask for my number?"

He chuckles, extending his phone to me. I type in my number and save my contact, then call myself.

"I'm turning my phone off until I leave here tomorrow," he says as I give it back to him. I feel very special.

"Cats," I say, still in disbelief about my search. He sits next to me on the couch, our shoulders brushing. Neither of us says anything, but the silence feels comfortable. I lean into him, and he puts his arm around my shoulder, giving me a little squeeze. "You may be the most interesting person I've ever met," I admit.

13

Patrick

The pressure of the last hour presses down on me—work, stress, chaos—but right now, sitting next to Rachel, I feel a sense of calm. I glance at her, still surprised she stayed. After everything, I wouldn't have blamed her if she'd bailed. But here she is.

"Can I take you out for dinner to apologize?" I ask, the words slipping out before I can overthink them.

Rachel turns to me. "You want to apologize?" Her voice is almost teasing.

"I do."

She bites her lip, holding back a laugh. "Are you into cold plunging?"

"No ..." *Where is she going with this?*

"Well, I think you can apologize by doing a polar plunge into the lake."

I raise an eyebrow. "So, you want to punish me?"

Her cheeks flush, her giggle soft but playful. "I want to know why you were talking to your CEO about penetration and backdoors ... and I also want to know how seriously you want to make up for the last hour."

The flirtation in her voice is impossible to miss. I'm caught between laughing and taking her seriously. Holding her gaze, I decide to lean into it, feeling bolder than I have all day. "Do you want to know that before or after I spoil you until you can't take anymore?"

Rachel's breath catches, her smile faltering as the heat between us builds. "Patch."

I freeze. No one calls me that except my close friends, and hearing it come from her does something to me. Something I wasn't prepared for. She bites her lip again, glancing out the window. "I'm going to need you to polar plunge first," she says, looking out at the lake.

I raise an eyebrow, feeling the pull of her challenge. "Is degradation your thing?"

She swats my arm, whispering, "Patch! Are you ... are you naughty?"

I smirk, running my fingers along my lips as I think about how far I can push this. "Am I polar plunging alone?"

She doesn't answer right away, her eyes searching mine. The playful atmosphere between us shifts. The tension between us isn't just about teasing anymore. Our attraction to each other is undeniable.

"Maybe," she finally says.

"I'm serious, though. Let me make it up to you. Dinner. No interruptions."

She tilts her head, her smile returning. "I'll consider this offer after you run into the lake."

"Do I get to keep my clothes on?"

She bites her lip, checking me out. "What do you think?"

"I think there are a lot of security cameras here ... so can I keep my boxers on?"

"Mmm ... I'll allow it."

"Are you joining me?"

"Mmm," she teases, snuggling into my chest. "Undecided."

I grab her jaw, staring deeply into her blue eyes. "Do you want me to beg you to join?"

14

Rachel

Patrick is a nerd in the streets and fucking nasty in the sheets, right?! Like casually using the word degradation. Vanilla people don't throw that word around. *How much more am I going to taunt him?* Am I going to run into the freezing cold lake with him? Am I going to fuck him? Too many questions are swirling in my mind. *Patrick Nowak.*

"I think you're into being punished," I whisper.

He bites his lip. "However you want it to go, kitten."

Kitten?! My jaw drops, and I let out a laugh, trying to process the shift. "Kitten?" I repeat, still reeling. "You've been holding onto that one, haven't you?"

He chuckles. Patrick's confidence catches me off guard, and I like it. The way he's shifted from that nervous, adorable guy to someone more sure of himself—it's messing with my head. Swinging my leg over to straddle him, I want to remind him that I'm in control. But he smirks, and now I'm second-guessing myself.

"Let's rewind," I say, placing a kiss on his lips. "I think you need to tell me about how you were almost a felon."

His hands land on my hips. "That's what you want to talk about right now?"

"It's that, or we go down to the lake and you can strip for me."

"You're demanding ... but I like it."

I raise an eyebrow, leaning in closer. "I like a few things about you too."

We kiss again, this time softer, sweeter. The kind of kiss that is distracting me from this playful back and forth.

"Okay ... the casino hack ..." He pauses, brushing my hair behind my shoulder. "It started off as a joke, honestly. But the deeper we got, the more we realized how bad their security was. It was like falling down a rabbit hole. One minute we're laughing, the next ... we're in way too deep."

I lean in, wanting to know everything. "And then?"

"Then we caused chaos. They lost millions, and we almost lost our freedom."

"I can only imagine how scary that was ... a prank almost turning into jail time."

"It would have been prison time. Fortunately, our legal team was able to convince them that we were all better off helping them than sitting in a cell."

It's silent between us until I can't hold back. "So, you're very familiar with back doors?" I smirk, truly feeling unhinged at how him being a nerdy bad boy is making me feel.

"One more than the other."

"Now I'm blushing." I swat his arm. "Why is everything about hacking so sexual?"

"Why are *you* making it sexual?" He pulls me in for a kiss. "I like you," he breathes between kisses.

"I like you too."

We stare at each other, both smiling. "Why am I turned on by you almost being a felon?" I whisper in his ear.

"You know why."

"Mmm," I tease, letting the moment linger between us.

"I'm never going to call you a good girl." He squeezes my thighs, his grip firm but teasing. "I think you're a kitten ... and I love cats."

I laugh, rolling my eyes. "Are you seriously making a pussy joke right now?"

"I'm making a 'you like to be taken care of' assumption."

I giggle, more nervously this time, because damn, if that isn't the fucking truth.

"I don't like you being the one in control."

"You sure?" he breathes, kissing my neck. "So ... what's next?"

More of this.

"You, in your boxers, running into the lake."

We hold a flirty stare, the challenge hanging between us. My heart races, and I'm caught between wanting to see him running into the freezing water and the pull of what's happening right here on this couch.

"Only if you join me."

I bite my lip, trying to decide whether I'm ready for that kind of plunge in more ways than one.

15

Patrick

"Do you know where the beach towels are?" I ask, trying to ease the tension that's lingered after Rachel avoided saying whether she'd join me in the lake.

She tilts her head. "So, you're actually going to do it?" she asks, her voice giddy with excitement.

Of course I am. If running into a freezing cold lake in just my boxers is what she wants, I'll do it. I'm more obsessed with her than I ever thought possible.

"I'll do whatever you ask."

She raises an eyebrow. "I like a good boy."

I smirk. "You're such a flirt. Show me the towels."

Rachel points. "There's a mudroom over there."

Biting my lip, my mind filled with things to say, I go for it. "You're either going in with your clothes or in your underwear."

"I'm not going in."

"You are."

"I'm not." The giggle that follows makes me think she wants it though.

"Well ... when I count to ten, I'm tossing you over my

shoulder," I say, raising an eyebrow. "Your choice on how much clothing you're wearing then."

She lets out a laugh, shaking her head in disbelief. "You wouldn't."

I start counting, slowly. "One ..."

Her eyes dart away, like she's weighing her options, then back to me. "You wouldn't," she repeats, though the edge in her voice suggests she's not entirely convinced.

"Two ..."

"You don't even have a towel yet."

As I open my mouth, Rachel swiftly dismounts and bolts down the hall, her laughter echoing through the house. I'm quick to follow her, running behind. By the time I catch up, she's already yanking open a cupboard, pulling out a couple of towels.

"Three ..." I tease.

"You first!" she squeals, looking down at my chest.

I toss off my shirt, and she bites her lip, checking me out. "Four ..." I say, serious about what is going to happen when I get to ten and loving her reaction to me being shirtless. "You should probably start getting undressed unless you want wet clothes."

She crosses her arms but smirks, and I step out of my jeans, standing there in just my boxers. "Five."

"Make me," she challenges, and I move closer to her, resting my hands on the top of her jeans.

"You want me to undress you?" I ask, hesitant and wanting to confirm.

She lifts her arms up in response and I slide her shirt over her head slowly, my fingers brushing the bare skin of her sides. Every second feels longer, and I have to force myself to breathe normally. *How is this even happening?*

"You're so beautiful." My fingers linger at the waistband of her jeans. "What about these?"

"I think they have to go." She smirks, then giggles. "Thank God I'm wearing underwear today."

I cock a brow, turned on, unable to speak and in disbelief about this day. I'm about to run into freezing water with the hottest, most playful, fun girl, both of us in our underwear. *She's amazing.*

The guys' warning from before pops into my thoughts. What if this is just fun for her, and I'm reading too much into it? What if I screw this up and ruin everything?

"Aren't you going to help me?" she challenges.

It hits me—*we might hook up*. Holy shit. I hide my face in my hands, trying to pull myself together. Kissing her has been epic, but ... *oh my God.* Focus. She wants me to take her pants off. Focus on the task at hand. *She wants* you *to take her pants off.*

My hands tremble a little as I unbutton her jeans. I can't look into her eyes right now. I'm too nervous.

"It's cute that you're nervous," she whispers. "I find it very charming."

"I ... I really didn't think this was going to happen today," I admit, staring into her amazing blue eyes before dropping to my knees to pull her pants down. "I was just hoping to talk with you."

"You're so sweet." She pats the top of my head as she steps out of her jeans. "And such a good boy."

I'm nervous, but there's a part of me—just beneath the surface—that wants to take control, to show her I'm not just the nervous guy she thinks I am. It's time to show her.

I bite the side of her hip on the way up and then whisper, "I know how to be bad."

16

Rachel

"Prove it," I challenge, locking my eyes on his, feeling a rush of anticipation. His boldness surprises me, and I'm reeling from how much I love it.

A mischievous grin spreads across his face, and before I can fully process, he throws me over his shoulder. I let out a scream, but it's not out of fear—it's pure excitement. There's no way I'm telling him to put me down. I don't want him to.

"Time for our cold plunge," he announces, grabbing the towels and opening the door.

"Patrick!" I squeal, laughing uncontrollably as he runs toward the lake.

I haven't felt this excited about a guy or done something so crazy like this in a long time. There's something different about him. The way he looks at me, I know he's genuine. He's not playing emotional games. He could have said no to this wild idea, but I'm glad he didn't. With him, I feel free, silly, and wild. I've been with confident guys before, but they always made me feel small in comparison. Patrick's confident too, but there's a sweet uncertainty in him, like he's surprised I even want to be here. It's endearing. He doesn't put on an act, and that makes me want to drop all mine too. I can be vulnerable with him without worrying about being judged. That's rare, and it's making me feel things I didn't expect.

"Here we go," Patrick says as his feet hit the water's edge.

The March air bites at my exposed skin, but nothing can prepare me for the plunge. The icy water slams into us, a shockwave coursing through my body. Every nerve jolts awake, the cold hitting like a punch, and I lose my breath.

My scream dies in my throat as I'm pulled under the freezing water. Every muscle tightens in protest. Patrick is right there, gripping my hand, pulling me up. I gasp for air, my lungs burning, my skin prickling with the cold.

"Fucking freezing," he stammers, his voice shaking as we stumble toward the shore, still holding hands. The water sloshes around our legs, but my body is too numb to feel it.

"Why do people do this willingly every day?" His teeth are chattering in sync with mine.

I can barely speak through the laughter, my body buzzing with the sheer thrill of it all. My skin feels raw, my hair sticking to my face, but I feel alive—more alive than I've felt in so long.

Patrick grabs a towel, wrapping it around me. The warmth is a relief, and I cling to it, trying to regain feeling in my fingers. He goes in for a kiss, and I smile, meeting his lips despite the cold. He's shivering too, grabbing the other towel for himself.

"I've never done that before."

I stand there, heart racing, staring at him. Adrenaline is still coursing through me, and I know exactly what I want next.

"Shower?"

He smiles, interlacing his fingers with mine. "There's one in my room ..."

We stumble through the door, dripping wet, still buzzing from the plunge. As I gather my clothes, the reality of being half-naked in my biggest account hits me. I glance down at myself—just a towel, hair dripping. This is moving fast, faster than I imagined. But when I catch Patrick's eye, all hesitation slips away. He's looking at me like he sees all of me, not just the girl in a towel. I'm too caught up in the thrill to stop now.

"We're just going to make out in the shower while we warm up," I tease, nudging him as we walk farther into the house.

But truthfully, I want more.

As we head upstairs, I clutch my towel tighter. It's strange—I've never felt this vulnerable. The playful banter, the teasing. It was fun. But now, nerves are kicking in. I'm confident, but deep down, I'm scared. Nothing about Patrick says he's a one-night-stand guy. And while I want to sleep with him, I know this is more than that. This is real.

Patrick's staying in a guest room overlooking the lake. He kisses my forehead before walking into the bathroom. I hear the shower turn on, and I take a deep breath. This was my idea. I smirk, following him in.

Leaning against the counter, I watch him. Removing the towel, I let it fall to the floor.

"I like you undressing me."

"You ... you—" he stammers, and it's so cute. "You want to be naked in the shower?"

"Of course."

His eyes dart down my body, and I feel so sexy as he checks me out in my underwear.

"Can I touch you?" he asks, unclasping my bra.

"Yes," I whisper, "but first, I really need to warm up." My bra drops, and he gets on his knees, kissing my lower stomach. When he bites the waistband of my underwear, my breath hitches.

"Patrick ..." I murmur as he pulls them down with his mouth. A smirk is glued to my face, watching him take off his boxers. I instinctively bite my lip at the sight of him.

"I'm surprised you're not harder," I tease.

"I'm freezing too!" He pokes me, then motions for me to enter the shower.

Even though the water is lukewarm, it feels like pins and needles against my skin. Patrick's hands rest on my hips. "I feel so comfortable with you," I share, surprised at how true it feels.

"Same ... although I'm still processing that you're into me."

"I'm very into you, Patrick," I say, pulling him into a kiss. "So, why are you single?" I run my hands down his back after we break apart.

"I don't put myself out there," he admits, taking my hands in his. "I was anxious about coming today. This is so unlike me."

"Being naked in a shower with a girl you just met?"

"Exactly ... uncharted waters." He chuckles, causing me to laugh at its truth and cuteness. Guiding me back under the water, he asks, "Why are you single?"

"The real answer to that is kinda long," I say, and he kisses my forehead. I smile before continuing. "From the time I was sixteen until I was twenty-five, I was with the same guy. After I called off the wedding, I wanted to live carefree. Date whoever. Sleep with whoever. I felt like I missed out on a lot." I pause, and he kisses me again. "But this party girl is tired now. I want something more."

Patrick's hands move back to my hips as he gently presses me against the shower wall. I love him towering over me. Holding my jaw in his hand, he stares deeply into my eyes. "I've never felt this way before."

17

Patrick

"Our connection," she whispers, holding my gaze as I brush my thumb along her jaw. "It's overwhelming."

"I know." My eyes lock onto hers before drifting lower. "You're so fucking sexy, and I've been wanting to kiss you here," I say, kissing the tattoo of the green lips I put on her neck.

"Didn't you mention something about touching me?"

"Are you warmed up now?"

She glances down at my growing erection. "Looks like you are."

"Well ..." I let my hand trail from her jaw down to her neck. "Maybe I should keep warming you up."

She giggles as I lean in to kiss her, my hand sliding lower until I cup her breast. I squeeze gently, slipping my tongue into her mouth. "What are your limits?"

"What do you mean?"

"I want to make you come."

"How?"

"First ... with my fingers." I trail my tongue down to her

chest, flicking her nipple before circling it. "Then ..." I move my tongue up her neck to her ear, my voice low. "I'll make you come with this." I slowly lick her ear.

She laughs lightly. "How could I say no to that?" Her hand finds me, gripping my cock. The steam thickens around us as we lock eyes. "How about I give you the best blow job of your life in between all that?"

"You're perfect, kitten."

She laughs, releasing me. "Is that really what you want my nickname to be?"

"You're playful, smart, and you love being touched. It fits."

"Fine ... I'll be your kitten."

I kiss her again, hoping one day she'll be my girlfriend. As the kiss deepens, my hands explore her body, grabbing handfuls of her ass. "I'm an ass guy," I murmur between kisses. "I'm obsessed with yours."

She smiles. "Don't ever shave your beard."

My hand glides up her thigh, slipping between her legs, and my thumb finds her clit. She flinches at the touch. "I want to make you feel good."

"You do."

"I want to hear you make sexy noises."

She moans softly and pulls me in for another kiss as I slide two fingers inside her. Rachel exhales, ragged, and I love how she feels as I slowly explore her.

"Fuck," she whispers, closing her eyes.

"I think we're the same kind of naughty," I whisper in her ear, watching as she bites her lip. "I'll be your good boy ... spoiling you, always. But I'll also be the guy who pins you against a wall and has my way with you."

Her eyelids flutter open. "So ... you're perfect."

"Not as perfect as you." I kiss her neck, speeding up the circles on her clit. "Do you want to come for me?"

"Yes."

"Close your eyes."

I watch her, captivated, as I increase the intensity, finger-fucking her deeper. Her face softens, lips parting slightly. "Rachel ... you are everything."

She shakes her head, and I crash my lips against hers.

"Listen to me ... you are fucking everything."

"Okay." I hear the disbelief in that response.

"Everything." I drop to my knees, changing course, flicking my tongue over her clit. "I can't wait any longer."

18

Rachel

Smirking, loving the feel of his fingers inside me and his tongue between my legs, I can't help myself. "Such a good boy."

His eyes flick up to mine, pure heat in them, as he grabs my leg and pulls it over his shoulder. *Shit.* This is epic. I love how his tongue feels, how his fingers stroke me, how his beard adds that extra sensation. Closing my eyes, I savor it all, feeling his hands gripping my thighs. Then one of his hands moves to my ass, squeezing, before he stands and hoists my other leg over his shoulder.

"Patch," I squeal, now draped over his shoulders as he continues eating me out. *I'm on his fucking shoulders!* His eyes meet mine, and oh my God. This is the hottest thing I've ever experienced. He wasn't kidding about being strong. I'm distracted by how utterly insane—and amazing—this is. We *are* the same kind of naughty.

Running my fingers through his brown hair, I can't get enough as his tongue moves faster, his rhythm intensifying.

"Shit," I pant, feeling myself get close.

He nods while he licks, and I'm smiling, still in disbelief that I'm on his shoulders, pressed against the shower wall.

"I'm going to come," I breathe, overwhelmed by every detail of this. His tongue shifts from circles to fast flicks. "Fuck," I exhale, biting my lip, too nervous to squirm on his shoulders, so I just tug his hair and press my back harder into the wall. He's relentless, fucking going at me. *Such a good boy.* I bite down on my lip and let out a loud, shaky exhale, right on the edge. His hands roam and squeeze, and I scream out, releasing with a shudder as I pulse against his tongue. He finishes with a few slow strokes, then grips my waist and lifts me down from his shoulders, placing me gently back on the shower floor.

"Um ..." is all I can manage, a schoolgirl grin spreading across my face. "That was the hottest thing ever."

His smirk is pure satisfaction. "I'm glad you liked it."

"I fucking *loved* it. I really like being manhandled like that."

"I had a feeling, kitten."

Our gazes lock, the air between us still thick with heat. I can't resist any longer and push him against the wall. My hand slides down, wrapping around his cock, loving how hard he is for me. The control shifts between us, and I revel in it.

Slowly, I stroke him, watching his expression. His head tilts back, eyes closing as he lets out a groan. *A younger man.* What a fucking thought. I could be dating a younger man. I want to be dating this twenty-seven-year-old—this man.

"You better come in my mouth," I say before dropping to my knees.

19

Patrick

"I'll do whatever you say," I manage. *This is the best day of my life.* Rachel smirks, sticking her tongue out before teasingly licking up my shaft. I shake my head, overwhelmed, loving everything about her and still buzzing from the thrill of having her on my shoulders. *That fantasy ... nailed.*

She devours me. *Shit.* Rachel is going to be perfect for all my fantasies, and I'm sure she has plenty too. My grip tightens on the hair at her neck, pulling her closer, loving the way her mouth feels wrapped around me.

She takes me deep, and with every inch, my obsession with her grows. Watching her, the way she moves, the way she takes all of me—this is everything. I wasn't lying when I said she was everything. I meant it.

"This is the best blow job of my life."

Her eyes flick up to meet mine. I can barely breathe. "Sexy," I whisper, utterly captivated. She's *worshiping* me, and I've never felt more wanted, more needed. Her tongue, her lips—fuck.

I've never believed in fate, not really. But *how else* could

I explain this? How the fuck would I have ever met her if it were not for this weekend?

A huff escapes me, the pressure building, tightening. I run my hand through her hair, knowing deep down I'll never get enough of this—of her.

"I'm right there," I breathe, my voice thick with need. She speeds up, her rhythm perfect. "Fuck, baby. This is so good."

Staring at her, fantasizing about a future with Rachel, I explode into her mouth. *Fuck*, that was intense.

20

Rachel

As I towel off and start to dress, Patrick's eyes linger on me, and I love it. I love how he looks at me. Pulling on my jeans, I ask, "How about instead of you taking me out for dinner, we order Chinese food and cuddle on my couch?"

His big smile is instant as he pulls his own jeans on. "Whatever you want."

I know he means it, that he's sincere, and I love that. "I want you to sleep over ... but I want us to wait to have sex. I don't want to rush that."

"I don't want to rush that either." He grabs my hand, yanking me in for a hug, and I rest my head against his chest, squeezing him tight. "Cuddling on the couch is exactly what I want to do with the rest of the evening," he says, playing with my hair.

"Go put your glasses on," I say, leaning back to stare into his green eyes. "I want you to be in max comfort mode at my house. So, actually ... you need to change. I want you in sweatpants and a hoodie too."

"Demanding, kitten." He kisses my forehead and steps

back into the bathroom. I flop onto the bed, a little smile glued to my face as I wait for him.

Those black plastic frames. "The glasses are a very hot vibe," I say when he reemerges.

"I can't wait to see you in your glasses."

He drops his jeans, and yup. Patrick's the living embodiment of my mood-boarded perfect man. Thick and strong, and my mind begins to wander.

"I cannot wait to be tangled up with you on the couch."

"Tangled?" He raises a brow, pulling on sweatpants and tossing on a hoodie.

"I'm a cuddle monster, so you will be begging for me to get off of you."

"Never," he says in a light laugh.

Patrick extends a hand as he approaches the bed, and I grab it. Hand in hand, we walk down the stairs.

"Let me tell Brandon about my plans."

I smile up at him, and we search the house until we find Brandon cooking in the kitchen.

He smiles seeing us, and his eyes fall down, looking at us holding hands. "Where are you two off to?"

"Rachel's place."

21

Patrick

Brandon extends a fist for a bump, and I release Rachel's hand.

"So proud of you," Brandon says quietly, tapping his knuckles into mine. His eyes have that look—I mean I got lucky, but not that kind of lucky that I think he's assuming. We smirk at each other until he says, "You need to be back by noon tomorrow."

"Sounds good." I nod, leaning against the kitchen counter. "Sorry we didn't get to hang."

"Dude, go have fun." He waves me off.

I glance at the stove where chicken breasts sizzle in a skillet. "Were you cooking for us?"

"Someone might be coming by." He shrugs, not looking directly at me.

I squint. "Who?"

"You know who."

"You two." Brandon and his on-again, off-again girlfriend Kate. They're confusing everyone, including themselves. In the year I've known Brandon, their relationship has been a rollercoaster. "I guess we both have a thing for older women."

Brandon raises his eyebrows, looking surprised to learn this fact about Rachel. "Well, it looks like my older woman wanted to get out of the city too. She's at her dad's place."

"Right. That's how you two met, summering up here."

"Enough about me. Get out of here already."

"Don't sleep with her," I whisper, knowing how that always restarts the "on" part of their relationship.

"I'll do my best." He winks. "Wear protection," he teases quietly so Rachel can't hear.

"Wear protection." I nudge him. Although I hope they don't get back together. He's so solid in his sobriety. She is not.

Brandon chuckles, pulling me in for a hug. Patting me on the back, he says, "Seriously, I'm excited for you. I have a good feeling about you two."

22

Rachel

We step outside, hand in hand, and I can't get this smile off my face. We keep smiling at each other, nudging into one another, and are generally being too fucking cute. After we slide into my SUV, I toss him my phone.

Buckling my seatbelt, I suggest, "Play me something you think I would like but have never heard before."

He strokes his beard, thoughtful. "You like emo and alternative music. Let me think."

I pull onto the road and feel at peace. I look back over at Patrick, and he winks at me. A song I've never heard begins to play. The beat is gentle at first, but when the vocals come in, I instantly love this song. Smiling, I bob my head to the beat.

"This is great!"

"I thought you would like it." He reaches for my hand, interlacing our fingers. "It's 'Wicked Ones' by Dorothy. She's badass ... like you."

"Badass?"

"Yeah. You're badass."

Blushing, I glance at him before refocusing on the road. The song continues in the background, but my mind is thinking about the way he makes me feel. Safe, special, sexy, and most of all, comfortable.

"You're emotionally available, right?" I ask, breaking the silence, although everything about him so far screams yes.

"Yes," he says, though there's a slight curiosity in his tone, like he's wondering why I asked.

"I want to be with someone who's ready for something serious."

"I want something serious."

Our eyes lock in a shared understanding. It's like we're dancing around the possibilities, but both of us are clear that this, whatever this is, is going somewhere.

We quickly enter downtown Lake Geneva and pass by High Five. Oh, how things can change in a few hours.

"We're only a couple of minutes from my place," I share.

"This is a nice town. I see why you like it here," he says, staring out the window.

I do like it here, and my mind jumps ahead, thinking about things it shouldn't. *Would I like living in Chicago? Would he want to live in a small town?*

"How many screens do you have in your office?" I ask, breaking the silence.

"Eight." He says it too nonchalantly.

"Eight?!"

"Yeah ... eight at the office and four at home. I change it up depending on what's going on. If we're being hacked, I prefer to live at the office, otherwise, I like to work remotely."

"So, you could work from Lake Geneva?" I ask, half-joking but not really.

"I could."

We share another look, the smiles on both of our faces growing.

"Working from Lake Geneva is going to mess up my minimalist thing," he says.

"Why's that?"

"I would need to get a car."

We smirk at each other.

"Well, don't impulsively get a car because of a girl you randomly met."

"I have hundreds of YouTube videos to watch before I consider buying a car. I like to nerd out about the pros and cons of things."

"I like that you're nerdy."

"I like that you're so cute."

"My cheeks are hurting. Stop making me smile so much."

"But I like your smile."

Stopping at the red light, I stare at it, daydreaming a little about how surreal all of this is. *Patrick Nowak.*

"You give me 'I smoke weed here and there' vibes."

Patrick laughs softly, running a hand through his hair. "I used to smoke a decent amount of weed and do shrooms here and there, but my company has a firm no-drug policy. They have amazing benefits, but we have to regularly test clean. So now, I just drink a little."

"Intense."

"Our CEO is intense, but he's a cool guy." Patrick pauses, then turns to look at me. "What are your vices?"

I smile, my eyes briefly trailing down his arm before meeting his gaze again. "A nice cocktail or a glass of wine ... you."

His laugh is rich and genuine, and he squeezes my hand. "You're definitely going to be one for me too."

I love how comfortable we are together. How we can be playful one moment and serious the next. The light turns green, and I ask, "What crypto should I invest in?"

He leans back, tapping his fingers lightly on the armrest. "The ones the mainstream doesn't know about yet. Like if you threw a hundred dollars into everyone that isn't one of the big ones, I'm sure one will make you a few thousand in a couple of years."

"So it's legit? It isn't, like, a scam?"

He turns his head slightly to look at me. "Isn't everything a scam?"

I laugh, but his question lingers. "What do you mean?"

"Trading our time for money ... that's why I'm motivated to retire early. I want to live the fullest life possible, not just spend it working."

"I'm sure you're very frugal, but what's one thing you splurge on?"

"Travel. Like when I'm on vacation, there's no budget. I'm just swiping away. Tomorrow isn't guaranteed, so in those situations, it's time to go all out."

The idea of him, free and unrestrained, makes me smile. "Sounds like you're fun to travel with."

"I am."

"When's your next trip?" I ask, curious now about the places he's been, the adventures he's had.

"Japan at the end of next month."

We lock eyes, the silence stretching between us, thick with an unspoken challenge. There's a flirty tension in the air, something unplanned but undeniably exciting.

"I'm not inviting myself on your Japan trip," I tease.

"Why not?"

I laugh, shaking my head. "We just met."

"You're the one that said this was fated."

"Fated? Did I say fated?"

"You said it without saying it ... about the bar and how it brings people together."

I can't stop the smile from spreading across my face. *He's got a point.*

"How about you come to Chicago next weekend, and if that goes well ... then you come to Japan with me."

The idea catches me by surprise, but the thought of it—seeing him again, maybe even traveling together—it's crazy, but I want it. I can't believe we're talking like this, but it feels right.

"I would like to see you in Chicago next weekend ... and we can pencil in Japan."

I bite my lip, trying to contain the excitement bubbling up inside me. "I have to return you by noon tomorrow?" I ask, changing the subject.

"You can return me whenever you're bored of me."

"That's not going to happen." He lets go of my hand and moves it to my thigh. I quickly stare down at it and then look back at his cute bearded, glasses face. "So ... let's bed rot all of tomorrow morning?"

"Goblin mode, snuggling with you ... sounds perfect." He squeezes my thigh, and I love it.

23

Patrick

"Your house is cute," I say as we pull into her driveway. It's a little ranch home.

"Thanks."

Rachel shuts off the car, and I pull her into me by the back of the neck. Kissing her, it feels electric. "It's been too long," I whisper as our lips part. I chuckle inwardly. I haven't kissed a girl in months, and now going ten minutes without a kiss feels too long.

She giggles, and I'm happy to bring her smile back.

"I'm guessing your house is going to be spotless," I say, opening my car door.

"I'm a bit of a clean freak."

"I think you're generally a little freak," I tease, nudging into her as we walk up to the side door of her home. She giggles, and then I ask, "Do you have any pets?"

"Nope. Just a couple of succulents."

"Good. I'm allergic to dogs."

"What would you have done if I had a dog?"

"Suffered through it."

"Right. Degradation." Rachel sticks out her tongue a

little, and I smirk at how her mind is always in the gutter. The quirkiness of her home immediately brings a smile to my face. I like that it's a hodgepodge of random stuff that somehow works.

"Are you into thrifting?" I look around at the mismatched dining chairs.

"I'm a Facebook Marketplace addict when I'm bored."

"I like the place." Sliding my arm around her shoulder, I squeeze her into me. "Glasses time," I whisper in her ear.

"Okay ... make yourself at home. Grab whatever you want from the fridge." She starts down the hallway, then looks back. "Meet you on the couch."

I love how comfortable we are with each other. Opening the fridge, I grab a flavored sparkling water and check out what she has. *Could she have any more cheese?* There's string cheese, cheese slices, sprinkle cheese, and cottage cheese.

"Rachel," I yell, amused. "I think you have a cheese problem."

"Says who?" she yells from down the hall.

"I know you're a Wisconsin girl ... but this seems—"

"If you don't like cheese, I'm going to return you to Brandon," she jokes, walking down the hall in the cutest cat-eye-shaped glasses, yoga pants, and a baggy T-shirt.

"I like cheese."

"Good. I was nervous for a second."

We smirk at each other.

"Cat eyes," I softly say, loving how freaking cute she is in her glasses.

"They're cute, right?"

"Very." I step toward her, resting my hands on her hips. "I knew you were a kitten."

Leaning down to kiss her, she swats my chest as our lips

meet. I'm a little surprised when Rachel wraps her arms around my neck, not letting me go. Her tongue is saying she wants this to be more than a make out. I squeeze her ass, and she arches into me. *So much for just cuddling.* Not that I'm complaining because I am not. Picking her up, Rachel's legs immediately wrap around my waist. "Couch or bed?" I ask, breaking our kiss.

"Couch," she breathes, and I walk us toward it. Laying her down, I hover over the top of her. *She's so beautiful.* Pulling up her shirt to just below her bra, I kiss up her stomach. She giggles each time my lips touch her skin.

"So ticklish." I kiss over to her sides, and she squirms. Her hands find their way under my hoodie and are exploring my back. "What does my kitten want?" I whisper in her ear before flicking my tongue around it.

"Another orgasm."

Pulling her yoga pants down, I get a wicked idea. Yoga pants in hand, I take her phone out of the side pocket, giving it to her.

"Call the Chinese place."

Taking my glasses off, I set them on the coffee table and begin kissing her inner thigh delicately.

"You're going to be down there while I'm on the phone?"

She sounds hesitant for once, and I smile. I don't say anything. Instead, I make circles on her thigh with my tongue.

"Patch," she breathes, her tone telling me she's not opposed to this idea. "What do you want?" she asks, and I look up, although Rachel is a blur without my glasses on.

"This." I flick my tongue on her clit.

She giggles. "I mean from the restaurant."

"You pick. Get a lot." I go back to lightly flicking my tongue, teasing her.

"I've never done this before."

"You better call them before I have you on the edge."

It's silent for a beat, and then I hear the ring sound coming from her phone. I want her to be so on edge. I don't want her to be able to order. Making circles with my tongue, I slide in a finger.

"Hi. I'd like to place an order for delivery," she says, far too collected.

Increasing the pressure of my tongue on her clit, she squirms. I grab her thighs, pulling them over my shoulders, holding her tight.

"I'd like to order ..." She pauses. The pause brings me so much satisfaction. I lift my tongue to give her a false sense of confidence. "Crab rangoon." I slam my tongue back into her, and she pauses, pulling my hair so hard. "Veggie egg rolls, beef and broccoli," she says so fast, squirming on my face. I slide in two more fingers and fuck her with force. "Chicken ..." She loudly exhales, and I love this. Rachel is so wet and tight and perfect. "Fried rice and orange chicken," she says, nearly winded. I roam my hand up her body and pinch her nipple.

"Twen—" She stops the word, and a couple seconds pass. "That works." She manages, flustered. "Credit card?" Her voice is nearly in a pant.

I pull back from her, grabbing for my glasses. I take the phone out of her hand and hold it between my ear and shoulder.

"Hi," I say into the phone and also to Rachel. "Are you ready for the credit card details?" I ask them and smile at her. Pressing her phone firmly between my ear and shoulder, I need both of my hands to finish her.

Rachel's biting her lip, tilting her head back as my thumb makes circles on her clit. It's so hot. I begin sharing my credit card details from memory. She grabs for a pillow as I pick up the pace of my fingers. After she covers her face, I grab it and throw it across the living room. She giggles, and I want her to come before I hang up.

"The address?"

Rachel extends her hand to get her phone back, and I shake my head. "Tell me," I mouth. She shakes her head. "Tell me," I command.

"One," she pants as I circle my thumb on her clit and pound into her with my fingers. "Five," she pants and then sharply inhales. "Two."

"One. Five. Two," I repeat into the phone. I smile, taking in all of the signs that she's going to come. I love staring at my squirming, panting kitten in her cat-eyed glasses. She's so frustrated and turned on. My smile turns to a smirk as she doesn't speak. I really want her to come before this order is placed.

"Walworth Street," she breathes.

"Walworth Street," I repeat into the phone. "Come for me," I mouth to her, and the voice over the phone says it will be twenty to thirty minutes. I hang up and set her phone on the table. "You were too good at holding back."

"I would never be able to order from them again if I had moaned or something."

"Well, give in now. I want to hear you scream."

I take my glasses off and go back between her legs. Licking and sucking, she relaxes into me. I want to hear her. I want to hear more of her noises. Rachel pulls my hair again, and all I want is for her to give in, to let go, to let me take her over the edge.

"I love your tongue," she pants in the sexiest voice. "I'm so close."

Determined, I keep going, giving her everything my tongue and fingers have to offer.

"Fuck," she breathes and then the sexiest fucking whimper comes out of her as she shudders before I feel her pulsing on my fingers.

Kissing slowly up her stomach, she lays limp on the couch. "Did I kill you?" I joke.

"Yes. Many deaths."

I chuckle, kissing up her neck, then I kiss her deeply. "I love spoiling my kitten."

She smirks, shaking her head. "I'm always going to laugh when you say that."

"I love when you laugh."

"Cuddle me," she says, extending her arms up. I nestle into the couch with her, and she wraps her arms and legs around me.

I smile, remembering how she told me this would happen, us being tangled up on the couch. She giggles and squeezes me tight. "Cuddle monster."

24

Rachel

"You're not going to touch a utensil," Patrick says, taking the Chinese food out of the plastic bags and arranging it on the coffee table.

"You want to feed me?"

"Yes. I'm not done spoiling you."

"I could get used to this."

"I want you to."

"I can't believe ..." I trail off, thinking about him eating me out while I was ordering. *So hot.* We're staring at each other, and I know he's waiting for me to continue, but now I'm lost, captivated by his green eyes through his glasses. They're so green. Not hazel at all. They are pure green. "Your eyes are incredible."

"So are yours." He grabs the chopsticks, lifting a piece of broccoli and extending it toward me. "What can't you believe?" I lean forward, teasingly sticking out my tongue before taking the bite. The saltiness of the soy sauce hits my tastebuds, making me smile. There's something so intimate about him feeding me.

"How you were going at me when I was on the phone."

He smirks, then looks down and takes a couple of bites.

"Don't pretend to be shy now."

He shakes his head, smiling, and extends the chopsticks to my mouth.

"After we're done eating ..." I cover my mouth, chewing. "I owe you."

"We don't have to be, like, even on that stuff."

"Well, I want to suck your dick."

Patrick's mouth opens like he's going to say something, but then he blushes a little before taking another bite of food.

"Why are you being shy?"

"I'm just really happy."

"Me too. So, what are you most looking forward to about Japan?"

"The food. I plan on eating my body weight in sushi." I giggle, and he playfully pushes my shoulder. "I also want to visit some temples and gardens." He lifts a piece of beef with the chopsticks and offers it to me.

"Are you seriously going to feed me the whole time?" I ask with a laugh.

"It makes me happy to take care of you."

I nudge my shoulder into him, enjoying the way he looks at me. Picking up a crab rangoon with my fingers, I press it to his lips. "I want to feed you too." He bites down, holding eye contact with me.

"Whatever you want," he says, chewing with a little smirk.

"I like that phrase."

He's not just saying it to say it. No one's ever made me feel this cared for, not like this.

"If we go to Japan, I'm paying for everything," he says casually after another bite.

"No way!" My heart skips, surprised by how serious he sounds.

"I have over a million credit card points." He shrugs like it's nothing.

"Like figuratively or literally?" I squint at him.

"Credit card points are a fun game. I have, like, thirty credit cards and read so many Reddit forums about how to maximize points and everything."

I laugh softly, loving how nerdy he is. "It's too generous." I'm reeling that he's serious about paying.

"I don't think so. I already have the hotels booked. The airfare would be with points. Those are the largest expenses."

My heart's racing. This isn't him flexing. Patrick's sincerity scares me a little.

"Let me pay for some of the sushi at least," I say, getting more excited about the idea of us going to Japan.

"Okay."

I giggle, the giddiness bubbling up. "What am I going to hate about traveling with you?"

He pauses, thinking. "Some people find it odd when I talk into a translation app and then have it speak for me in public."

"That's not so bad. How do you handle when a flight gets canceled or a major delay happens?"

"I roll with it." Staring into his eyes, I believe him. "Usually, I open my laptop and try to find alternative routes or plans."

"So I get to be a passenger princess the whole time?" I smirk, continuing to lean into the idea.

"Yes, kitten."

"I'm warming up to this whole kitten thing."

Patrick kisses me softly. The kiss feels like a promise. Like we're going to Japan.

We continue to banter, feeding each other between smiles and laughs until I find myself resting my head in his lap, gazing up at him. The moment is quiet, peaceful, and I feel completely at ease.

"Today is the best day."

"I agree." His fingers are gently combing through my hair. His touch is soothing, keeping me at peace with the world.

But I want to make sure we're on the same page. I hesitate but then ask the question lingering in the back of my mind. "So, you want to, like, do this ... be in a long-distance thing?"

He doesn't answer right away. Patrick holds that same steady gaze until I squint at him, half-smiling. It's crazy to try and put a label on what we're doing, but I also need to know. We're flirting with a lot of things right now.

"If you want to put a title on this or agree to some boundaries, I'm open. Know that you're the only one in my life."

I let out a breath I didn't realize I was holding. "I don't have a roster, trust me." I laugh. "But ... yeah ... let's not hook up with anyone else."

"What else do you want?" His heartfelt voice pulls me in further. I know, deep down, he'd give me anything right now.

I take a breath, surprised at how easy it feels to be vulnerable with him. "I want you to FaceTime me every day when you're done with work."

"Sounds good." The smile on his face. I love it. "Are you usually done cleaning by six each day?"

"I'm usually done by three. I start early and don't work, like, a full eight hours."

"When you come to visit next weekend, are you thinking you'll come by on Friday? I can take the day off."

I smile, feeling excitement bubble up again. "How about I show up on Thursday night?"

"Before or after dinner?"

"We could do a later dinner together?"

"That would work." His eyes light up as he adds, "I'll reserve a spot for you in my building to park."

"Three nights together," I whisper, smiling at him.

"I'm very excited."

"I'm sure ... you get to fuck me."

He blushes again, and I like making him nervous.

"Two hours is a long drive for a booty call."

"Patch can be sassy." I smile, staring at him, and he pulls his wallet out of his sweatpants pocket.

"Here," he says, taking out the fifty-dollar bill we got from our pull tab winnings. "For gas."

"I can pay for my own gas."

"Why not let the bar pay for the gas?"

Witty. "I think if the weekend goes well, you're going to have a girlfriend."

25

Patrick

Staring into Rachel's blue eyes through her glasses, I want her to be my girlfriend, to join me in Japan, to be by my side for all of it. I've traveled solo plenty, but this time, I want to experience everything with her.

Fate. I never gave it much thought before, but now ... maybe there's something to it. As I comb my fingers through her hair, I'm struck by how comfortable I am. How at ease I feel with someone I just met. I was so apprehensive this morning, my anxiety almost kept me at home. I almost didn't leave. What if I hadn't? I could've missed out on her.

"You're perfect," escapes my lips before I can stop it.

"You say that now." She giggles. "But I think you're perfect too." Then she squints at me. "Why did you and your last girlfriend break up?"

I chuckle, suddenly self-conscious for a new reason. "I haven't had a girlfriend in five years."

"Yeah?"

"We met a couple of months before the casino hack and ..." I trail off, deciding if I'm really going to get into all of this. It's definitely not a fun or flirty topic.

"What happened?" she asks, sitting up on the couch and grabbing my hands.

"I wasn't in a good place during all of that. I was really depressed, thinking my life was over."

"Oh," she says softly and wraps her arms around me. Her hug surprises me, but I lean into it, feeling her hold me tight. I wasn't expecting this to be her reaction, but it makes me smile as I hold her.

"Yeah," I say, as we continue to hug. "I kinda shut down."

Rachel squeezes me tighter. "I can relate, kinda. After I called off the wedding, I felt like I'd let everyone down, including myself. I was lost and had to figure out who I was."

We hold each other for a while. There's something about her presence that feels perfect, needed. I lean back and cup her jaw, my thumb running back and forth on her bottom lip.

"I think we should snuggle in bed," Rachel softly says.

I nod and start closing up the leftovers.

"So," Rachel's voice carries from the kitchen as she grabs some of the containers, "did that time start your love of alternative music?"

I smile, joining her. "I was a little emo before then, but yeah, it definitely increased my interest."

"I've always been a little emo."

I hand her the remaining containers, and she slides them into the fridge. Then she lifts her arms up, a big, playful smile spreading across her face.

"Carry me."

I chuckle. "You can't walk now?"

"I like when you carry me."

I like carrying her. "Which room is yours?"

"Last one on the left."

I scoop her up into my arms, and she giggles, nestling her head against my chest. "I really like you."

"Same."

I toss her down on the bed and look around her room. "This feels minimalist," I tease, noticing the blank walls and the Scandinavian decor.

"I find it calming." She crawls under the covers and pats the bed beside her.

"It is a calming space." I join her under the covers, and she cuddles into my chest.

"Do you ..." She pauses, and I squeeze her, my way of encouraging her to continue. "Have you ever been depressed since then?"

"A little," I admit, staring up at the ceiling. "When it starts to impact my day to day, I talk to someone."

"Well, I'm in therapy too, so don't feel weird about it."

"Yeah?"

"Lots of shit. Childhood, anxiety, everything."

I smile and kiss her forehead, appreciating the honesty.

She squeezes me, giggling into my chest. "Not exactly great foreplay conversation."

While hooking up again would be epic, this time we're sharing. I don't want it to end. "I want to get to know you more than anything else."

Rachel shifts, rolling on top of me, and kisses me gently. Her kisses start to escalate, and as much as I want this, I also want to slow down.

"Rachel ... how about we just talk?" Her eyes dart between mine. *She's nervous?* "We have next weekend to do nothing but be all over each other," I reassure.

She giggles. "You promise?"

"I fucking promise."

We lie there, talking for hours about everything—bands, pop culture, conspiracy theories, pet peeves. It's effortless being with her. And with each new topic, I fall deeper. By the time we drift off to sleep, I can't wait for her visit to Chicago next weekend and what's hopefully next for us. I'm imagining our life together, imagining what it would be like to do this every night. To have her by my side, to keep learning everything there is to know about her.

26

Rachel

Sunday, March 16th

Waking up next to Patrick, I catch the soft rise and fall of his chest. *He snores.* I giggle hearing his light snoring. The sight of him, so relaxed and peaceful in my bed, brings a smile to my face. I lean in and kiss his forehead gently as I replay all that happened yesterday.

Fate. The word floats through my thoughts again. It's funny how things line up, how one small change could have kept me from Patrick. If we hadn't brought back our ugly Christmas sweater tradition last December ... if Nicholas hadn't bought the bar ... if we were not running late on the clean ... if so many little things hadn't happened, I never would have met Patrick, let alone invited him to High Five. And I'm so glad I did.

When was the last time I looked at my phone? My friends are probably dying for an update. I slide out of bed and make my way to the living room. Picking it up from the coffee table, I begin a text to the BFF group chat as I walk back to my bedroom.

RACHEL WAGNER

To conclude our little tradition ... while there was no "shamrockin" last night, I think it's safe to say "I'm here for the Paddy" and am currently watching him sleep.

SARAH ANDERSON

Not creepy at all, but OMG!!! I'm so excited for you and St. Pat!

RACHEL WAGNER

We're spending next weekend together in Chicago too.

EMILY BROWN

Trifecta!

I hold in a laugh, not wanting to wake Patrick. He stirs a little as I make my way back under the covers but stays asleep. Next weekend. Chicago. I'm so happy. It's still new, but there's something about him—about us. I put my phone on my nightstand, settling back into the comfort of his chest, my mind drifting between excitement for what could be and this perfect moment. Our friend group is about to have no single friends.

The End

Review Page

Do you want to help the author get more recognition?

Please review this book!

Review via: Goodreads.com

Or via your purchase platform!

About The Author

Writing under the pen name, Serena Pier is a wine lover, coffee snob & wife. With Midwestern roots, her stories are primarily set in and around Chicago. Serena is deeply fascinated by power dynamics; her stories always explore unequal social status.

Thank you for reading *Shamrock Kisses: A High Five Novella*. It's the third in a series of three holiday themed novellas featuring Rachel and her friends Sarah and Emily.

Check out other books in Serena Pier's Geneva Lake's Universe at www.SerenaPier.com.

Follow Serena Pier on TikTok and Instagram:
@SerenaPierWrites